The Most Pleasant Festival of Sacrifice

Little Batul's Eid Celebration

Published by Tughra Books
345 Clifton Ave., Clifton,
NJ, 07011, USA

www.tughrabooks.com

Illustrated by Beyza Soylu
Graphic Design by Murat Özbayrak

ISBN: 978-1-59784-294-5

Printed by
Çağlayan A.Ş. Izmir, Turkey

The Most Pleasant Festival of Sacrifice

Little Batul's Eid Celebration

Munise Ülker

Illustrated by Beyza Soylu

Snowflakes were falling gently, and the holiday season was already in the air. Batul and Murad had so much fun making a snowman that morning. Since it was Sunday, their dad was taking the family to a close friend's house.

This was the house of their best friends Aysun and Ali, and it was only ten miles away. They were so excited and kept asking, "Are we there yet?" Batul is a second-grader and Murad has just started preschool. It was a tough winter this year; they had three days of school closings already because of the snow.

While her dad was driving Batul kept looking at the decorations on the streets and in front of neighbors' houses. There were a lot of decorations at the stores, too. It was very exciting that year: Christmas, Hanukkah and Eid ul-Adha — the Festival of Sacrifice, were around the same time. But Eid will fall on a different date next year, since it comes eleven days earlier every year.

Looking at the decorations outside, Batul started talking. "Mommy, I know what people do at Christmas; my friends told me at school. Santa comes to their house and they put presents under the Christmas tree. Santa brings them presents if they are good during the year. They open them up in the morning...."

Her parents looked at each other for a minute, they did not know what to say. It was right around Christmas time and Batul was excited to see all the decorations in the stores and her friends' houses. She just wanted to talk about it.

Then her mom said, "OK Batul, it's great that you know how your friends celebrate Christmas and welcome the new year. But you also know that we do not have a tree and we don't observe Christmas or the new year at our house, right? Can you tell me what we do at Eid ul-Adha and Eid ul-Fitr right after the fasting of the month of Ramadan?"

Batul paused for a second, trying to put her words together to remember what they did last year.

She said, "We buy new clothes, we go to the mosque in the morning and we give presents to each other. I also like the Eid Prayer, everyone coming together and praying to Allah for goodness, peace and happiness for everyone... It's really enjoyable and fun. I love it.

Then remember Mom, when we went to Turkey last year, we went to all the houses of our relatives. I can't even remember how many…They were all very happy to see us. We exchanged the Eid greetings and kissed the hands of our grandparents, aunts, uncles, and other elder relatives as a sign of respect. They kissed us back on our cheeks and gave us money or candy. We also went to see a shadow play performance. We loved it. Can we go to Turkey again daddy, please? It is not as much fun here at Eid time…."

Her mom thought about it, then said, "We'll see, inshaAllah." But she knew it would be really hard to go again. They just went there last year and they may not afford to go again; airplane tickets were expensive.

Batul's brother started cheering, "Yay! I want to go, too. I want to go, too."

They arrived at their friend's house; it was a short ride anyway. Batul and Murad were very happy to see their friends. They brought a game to play, too. They flew upstairs to play it right away.

The dads started a lively discussion over a book they had read, and the moms were cutting lettuce for the salad. Batul's mom was very quiet. She was thinking about what Batul said in the car. So she decided to open up and discuss this with her friend.

She said, "Maryam, I love being in the States; I love my job, friends, and neighbors here. Of course, it is hard to be away from all of the relatives, especially my mom, dad and my sister. Yes, they did come to visit us a couple of times, but especially around the religious festivals it gets tougher to be away. And I am afraid my children won't have these great memories about Eid celebrations as they grow up, away from their own culture and values. It is fantastic that they learn about all different cultures and peoples here, but what can we do to help them to learn their own values?"

"You do send her to the weekend school still, right?" asked Maryam.

"Yes, sure. She memorized many short surahs already, doing great. But I remember my childhood, how excited we would be when it was Eid ul-Adha!"

"What do you say we do something special this year?"

"Like what?"

"Let's give them their best Eid celebration ever. They can tell this to their children years later," she smiled.

"Mmm, aren't you a good party planner? What do you have in mind?"

"Well, first of all we have a lot of Muslim families around here. We can also ask our non-Muslim neighbors if they would like to join us."

"OK."

"I'll call a couple other moms over tomorrow evening after work. We'll talk, OK?"

"Great."

It was the perfect cold winter day, beautifully bright and sunny. They started eating lunch. Murad kept telling everyone to wash their hands before eating.

The neighborhood mothers got together the next day. They decided what they could do to surprise the children and then divided up the various tasks. They also wanted to get the community involved—they decided to ask kids living at an orphanage to come to the celebrations.

Every Muslim family would be responsible for buying new clothes for two children from the orphanage, and they would take their own children along to do the shopping. This would be a great way to thank Allah for everything we have and teach the children both the importance of sharing and being a part of the community.

When Batul and Murad went back home, they got Eid cards ready for their grandparents. Batul helped her brother with his Eid card, and then each mailed their postcards to Turkey. They knew this would make their grandparents very happy.

The next day, Batul's mom called the local library and asked to be allowed to decorate a library bookcase with items describing the Muslim religious traditions. Muslim kids coming to the library would be very happy to see that. Such a display would make it easy to explain to their friends what Muslims do during this holiday.

13

Murad helped his mom carry items for the bookcase
to the library. The display looked beautiful.

It was only a week to Eid ul-Adha. That Saturday their teacher at the weekend school did a project with them. Each student made two presents—one to give to a friend in their class, and the other to another child in need in the community. Their parents were also going to give some of their Zakat, or prescribed alms, to the needy family. Batul knew how to do finger-weaving, so she made a scarf for Zaynab.

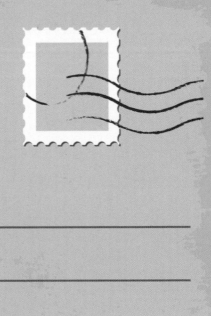

Batul and Murad also made Eid cards for their neighbors' kids to give along with some candy. Zaynab and Batul really enjoyed getting candy past Halloween, and they thought Eli and Nadia would enjoy their candy, too. Murad signed his name on the card himself. They were also excited to share and tell them what the Festival of Sacrifice is.

Batul's father had already told them that they celebrate Eid ul–Adha, or the Festival of Sacrifice, in remembrance of Prophet Abraham's readiness to sacrifice his son Ishmael to Allah the Almighty. He had also said that on Eid ul–Adha Muslims offer domestic animals as sacrifice, such as goat, sheep, cattle, and camel. This sacrifice of animals is made in order to pay a tribute to Prophet Abraham, since he was ready to fulfill the command of Allah the Almighty, Who gave him a sheep to sacrifice instead.

It was now the morning of Eid. They put their new clothes on. Murad thought he looked really cool with his new hair style. They went to the mosque to perform the Eid Prayer, and then they celebrated each other's Eid.

After the mosque, Murad and Batul called their grandparents to wish them Eid blessings. Murad's grandpa answered the phone. He was so happy to hear Murad's voice.

He said, "Murad, Eid Mubarak to you, too. We just got the Eid postcards you mailed us, they were beautiful. We are showing them to all the neighbors and relatives coming to visit us."

20

Grandpa's voice was a little shaky—he was glad that Murad couldn't see the tears in his eyes from missing his grandkids so much. He wished that he could fly to them right now. Then he said, "InshaAllah, Grandma and I will come and visit you next year with Eid gifts for you all!"

"This would be wonderful, indeed," said little Murad.

After the adults got some sheep and cattle sacrificed in a local farm, they made meat stew for everyone there. They also saved some of the meat to be given to their neighbors and the needy in their community.

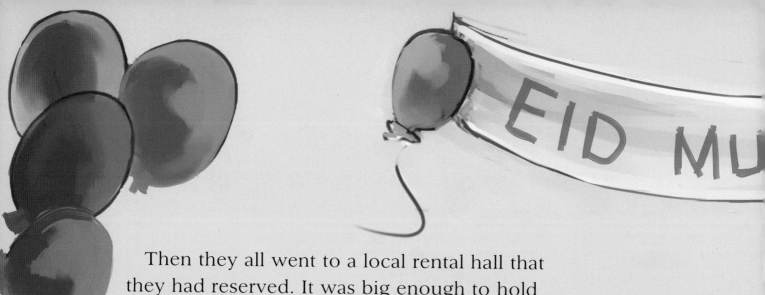

Then they all went to a local rental hall that they had reserved. It was big enough to hold everyone. They paid $5 admission and they also brought some food to share. Indeed, everybody brought a dish when they came—they also had plenty of meat stew, rice, and desert.

After everything was ready, the kids from the orphanage came in two buses. The kids greeted them at the door, gave them hugs and their presents. The shine in their eyes was priceless. Batul bought clothes for Clara, and Murad bought for Danielle. Clara was happy that she got a shirt in her favorite color—purplc.

While they were still eating a clown arrived. All the moms and dads gave additional presents to all of the children.

Zaynab loved the paint set she got from her dad. She would start painting as soon as she got home.

Then they started kissing the hands of their parents and grandparents and then the other elderly people there. They kissed them back and gave them allowance or candy. "I am rich," Ahmed thought, smiling when he got $2 from Zaynab's mom.

There was a piñata at the corner for little ones. Everyone took turns trying to break it, and Cal-ib got lucky. Boy, what chaos it was when it was broken. Ahmed was able to get three pieces of candy!

It was a lot of fun. They enjoyed seeing all their friends together at the same time.

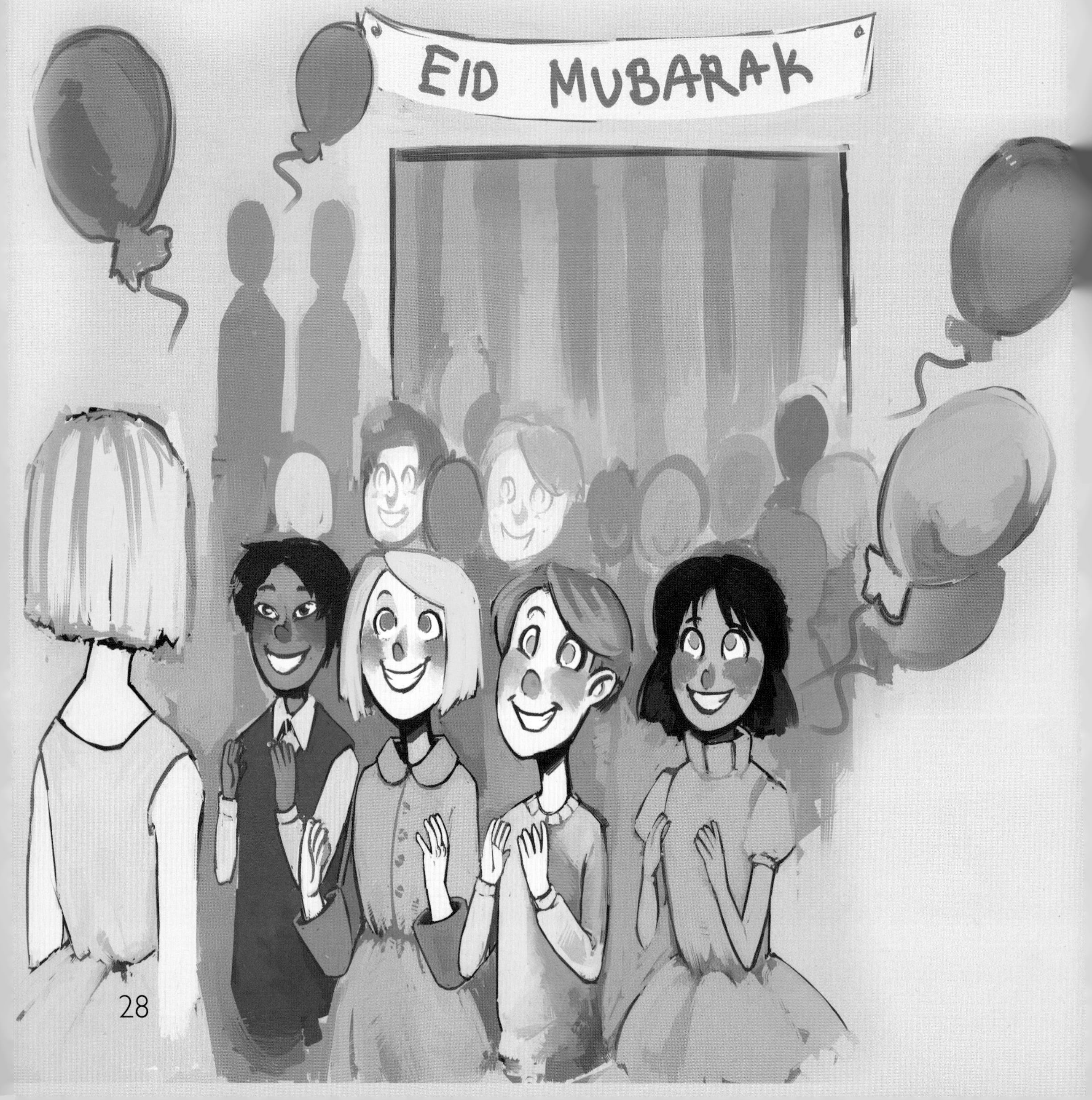
EID MUBARAK

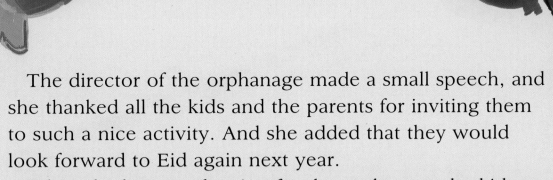

The director of the orphanage made a small speech, and she thanked all the kids and the parents for inviting them to such a nice activity. And she added that they would look forward to Eid again next year.

When the bus was leaving for the orphanage the kids got sad. They never wanted to leave the fun and their new friends. So they promised to visit each other again.

Batul and Murad were asleep in the car in five minutes. They were happy but tired. Right before closing her eyes Batul said, "I'll tell my teacher as well as my classmates, Eli and Nadia, about this Eid celebration. It was fantastic. Thank you Mom and Dad. I hope all the kids in the world will be as lucky as I am. And I hope next year Grandma and Pops will come, too. I will always remember this Eid!"

Notes

Notes

Notes